This Book Belongs To:

Freebird Publishers
Box 541, North Dighton, MA 02764
Info@FreebirdPublishers.com
www.FreebirdPublishers.com

All Freebird Publishers titles, imprints and distributed
lines are available at special quantity discounts for
bulk purchases for sales promotions, premiums,
fund-raising, educational or institutional use.

ISBN: 9781703426885

Printed in the United States of America

THE WISE JEWELER

WRITTEN & ILLUSTRATED BY
DELRON ERIC WHITE, JR.

Once upon a time...

there was a Jeweler who possessed some of Earth's most precious stones. She traveled far and wide, night and day. By land, and by sea to acquire these wonders of the world.

Astonished with her treasures, the Jeweler wanted nothing more than for the people to be able to witness the remarkable beauty bestowed upon Earth's rocks. So, she made out a sign, placing them inside a window sill, allowing everyone to watch.

And just as the Jeweler suspected, the people passing by the window stopped and stared outside in awe - mesmerized by the rocks' vibrant colors and smooth textures. They pointed and waved, wished and craved...that they too could possess some of Earth's most precious gems.

JEWELRY STORE

But there was one rock in particular who no one paid any attention to. His surface was dirty and it had no shine to it. The people laughed and called it bad names, causing the one in particular rock to feel so ashamed.

Even the other gems were not nice to him. They made him feel unworthy and twice as less.

"I'm Ruby! And I'm going to sell for a million dollars," one rock bragged with confidence.

"I'm Emerald! And I'm selling for a million too," proudly said the second.

"Well I'm Sapphire! And I won't say I'll sell for a million dollars but I'm guaranteed to sell for more than this mud ball," spoke the third rock as it pointed at the in particular rock.

With tears in it's eyes the in particular rock stared at the other three who had bursted into laughter. Not fully understanding the amount of pain and humiliation they were causing.

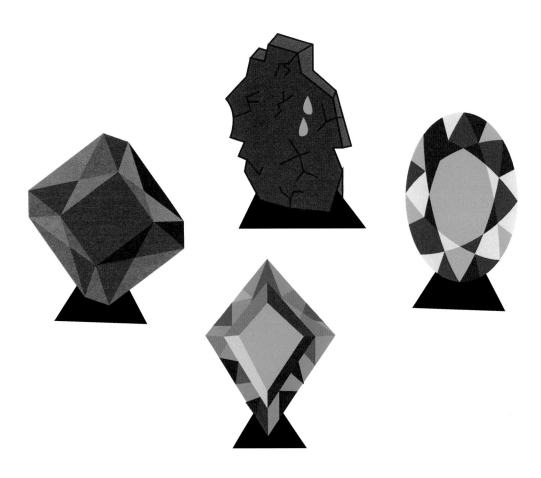

Filled with hurt, shame and confusion of not knowing it's name the in particular rock eased away, distancing itself from the others.

One day as the Jeweler was passing by the window she noticed the in particular rock all alone, not sitting next to the other gems, rejoicing, as they sang a song.

  My name is Ruby, my color is red.
I love to dance. I love to sing.

 My name is Sapphire, my color is blue.
I love to dance and sing too.

  My name is Emerald, my color is green.
I love to dance. I love to sing.

Curious as to why the in particular rock was so distant from the others, the Jeweler stopped at the window sill.

"Hey! What's the matter? Why are you so distant from the others, not singing the happy song?" she asked the in particular rock.

"They don't like me. Nobody likes me. I'm different. I don't shine like the others," the in particular rock answered."

"What do you mean? Don't you know that you're a gem too?" she replied.

"Yeah, an ugly mud rock whose outside has no color to it. I don't belong with the others. You were better off leaving me where you found me."

Hurt from the thought of the in particular rock's words, the Jeweler took him into her hands. With love and compassion she held onto him tight as they set sail, enroute to a different sight.

Once they reached where they were going, the Jeweler sat the in particular rock down on her desk, as she opened up a drawer removing a box, preparing to give him a special kind of test.

The Jeweler opened the box allowing what was inside to be seen.

The in particular rock's eyes twinkled with a beam as he stared at the strangest gem he had ever seen.

It was nothing like the others whose colors were red, blue and green. This gem was brown, still it was as beautiful as could be.

"His name is Diamond," the jeweler introduced to the in particular rock.

"Wow! He's beautiful," the in particular rock said staring mesmerizingly at the diamond.

"He is. Just like you," the Jeweler complimented them both.

Within an instant the in particular rock filled with doubt, as it turned away from the diamond to pout.

"No I'm not. You only say that to make me feel better. I'm not smooth and shiny on the outside like the others. And I'm definitely not unique as him."

"Look at me!", the Jeweler said. "What good is it to have a colorful, smooth outside when the inside is jagged and rough?"

The in particular rock couldn't be heard as it searched for an answer to the Jeweler's words.

"I'm going to teach you what it takes for you to be your best. All you have to do is listen, be obediant and before you know it, you too will shine like the rest." the jeweler promised the inparticular rock.

For weeks and weeks the Jeweler put the in particular rock through a series of tests where he gained a new understanding of life and was becoming his true self.

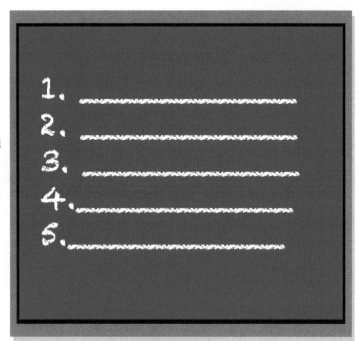

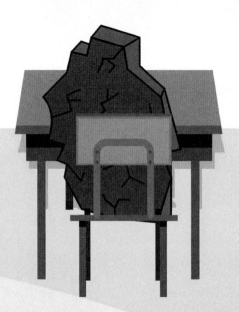

The more and more the in particular rock learned, the less and less he began to feel hollow. As he familiarized himself with the steps the Jeweler asked that he follow.

FORMAT

1. Always put God first.

2. Always love and never hate.

3. Always have patience and respect pressure.

4. Know your worth.

5. When it's your time to shine do so with moderation.

BEFORE   AFTER

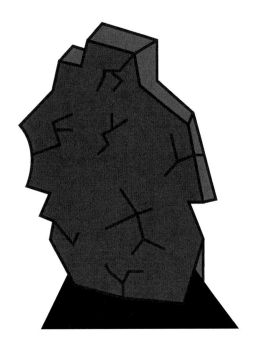 

And before he noticed, the once in particular rock who was covered with dirt, revealed something different, a true beauty from Earth.

The jeweler could not have been more happier for him then to witness Earth's wonder evolve into a gem. But the lesson wasn't over, there was one last test as she was preparing to take him back to the window sill to be with the rest of the gems.

Before leaving the gem inside the window sill with the rest,
the Jeweler wished him the best. Gave him her blessings and
reminded him of the lessons.

With the Jeweler now gone, the gem was on his own. As he took a few deep breaths staring around the window sill thinking that's where he belonged.

Within seconds the other gems surrounded him, questioning who he was and where the Jeweler had found him.

"Who are you? Where'd you come from?" Ruby asked.

"I'm the ugly mud rock who you all disliked," the gem answered.

"No way! You're beautiful" said Sapphire.

"You changed," spoke Emerald.

"No! I really didn't. This has always been me. I just never knew my full potential. You all, along with the Jeweler helped me. I'm a Diamond," he said proudly for the first time.

"Wow! Can you teach us how to reach our full potential?" Ruby asked impressed.

"Sure," Diamond insisted.

Ruby, Sapphire and Emerald all gathered close to hear Diamond speak. As he shared with them the knowledge the Jeweler taught him to reach his peak.

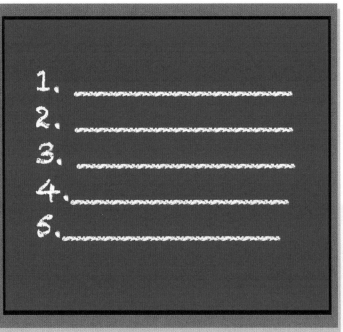

1. _____
2. _____
3. _____
4. _____
5. _____

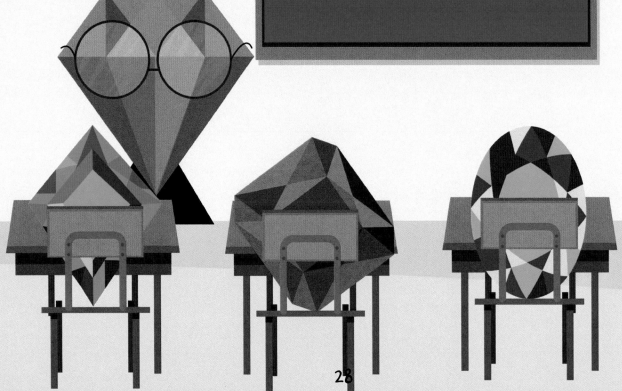

Thanks to the Jeweler and her lesssons, the gems were able to see that regardless of how we appear on the outside, on the inside we're all unique.

The End.

Author's Note

Children! Or shall I say The Future? I created this story with hopes of teaching you all the importance of having humility for one another, Regardless of how different one may appear on the outside, on the inside there's a uniqueness to you all that God designs for your individuality. There's no limit to who you can become. Never give up...Aim for the stars. If you miss...Well, there's still a chance of hitting the moon!

Much Love,
Delron White

Made in the USA
Coppell, TX
16 August 2020